The Story of Spot, the School Cat
Written by Diane Brookes
Illustrated by Stephen Lewis

for Spot

and all the other Northern cats
who eventually learn that spring follows Winter
and kids and cats come out to play once more

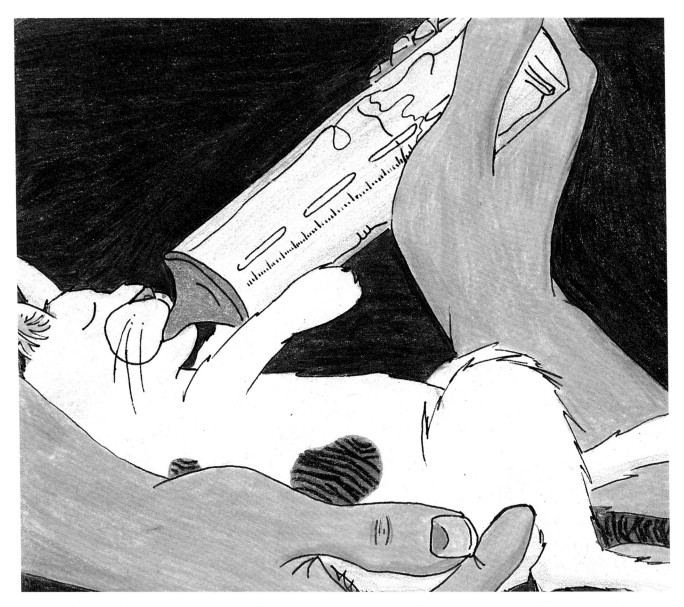

The first thing I remember is warm hands stroking me and wiping my face, a soft voice crooning and warm milk in my belly. Day by day those hands and voices came and went around me.

Sometimes the hands were big and sometimes small; sometimes the voices were soft and low and sometimes loud and happy. But always those hands and voices made me feel good.

As I grew older and opened my eyes I realized that the hands and voices belonged to people, big and small, who were always ready to pet me, cuddle me and play with me.

But one day all the people left the house. I looked everywhere but there was no one to cuddle me and only the other cats to play with. 'Where had they gone?' I wondered. A very long time later they were back.

In curiosity one morning I slipped out the door with the smallest of the people and followed her. She led me to a marvellous place – a place full of people, big and small!

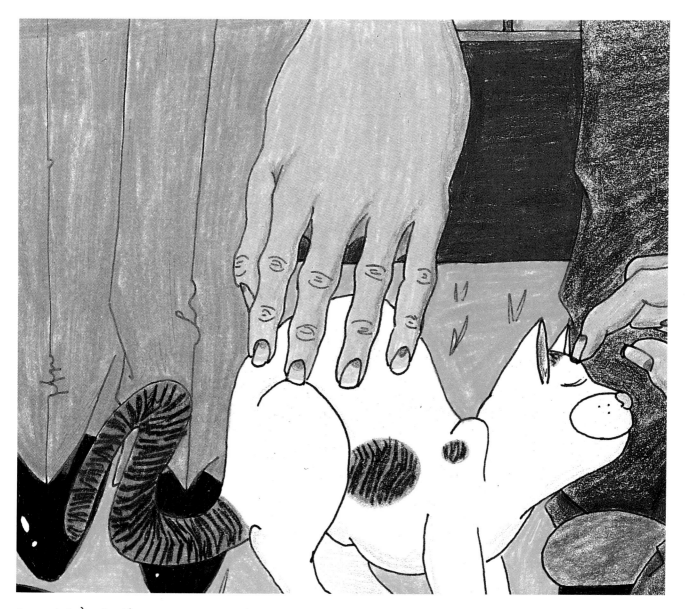

I couldn't believe my eyes! The small people looked at me and laughed. I ran to them and they cuddled me! I had found the greatest place in the world!

But now it is cold, the ground is white and I can't go outside anymore.
I miss my friends and playmates. I sit at the window and watch them
go by. They wave at me, but it's not the same.

Oh, how I wish I could go back to the great days when it was warm; when I could run outside to that marvellous place full of friends.

The End.